I0591113

YOU ARE EVERYTHING

10 Starter Stories

by

CEDRIC BROWN

You Are Everything

Ebook © 2020, Print © 2025

ISBN Print: 978-0-9857006-6-9

Ebook: 978-0-9857006-5-2

Because #BlackLivesMatter

PREFACE

For ten consecutive mornings in these strange times, I woke up and wrote a story snippet on my phone, usually while lying in bed. Inspired by my new discovery of flash fiction, this creative exercise made me quite happy—the voices of the characters who spoke to me in the morning frequently stayed with me all day.

I decided to trim each of these snippets to exactly 500 words before sharing them with others. This succinct form is much more suitable to me, a poet at heart, than standard length stories. None are meant to be complete tales, just a jumping off point for more imagining. That's the power of storytelling, however brief.

Cedric Brown
Winston-Salem, North Carolina
May 2020

P.S. August 2025

I wanted a printed version of this work, hence this 2025 edition. Most everything is the same as in the e-book, except for the added photos and a few extra paragraph breaks.

These are still strange times.

ONE

I was sitting on the front porch steps minding my own business, as I usually did on thick summer days, heat simmering into the evening. My stomach twanged a bit when I saw Trae coming down the sidewalk with his typical strut, both slightly pigeon-toed and bowlegged.

"Hey," he called out as he started across our small front lawn, making tracks in the grass I'd just cut the day before.

"Hey Trae."

He sat down with a loud exhale—Aahhhh—like he'd been on his feet all day—doing what, I don't know. He propped his arm on the uppermost step and leaned into the pose.

"Whatchu doing?"

"Nothin' really. Chillin'."

"Y'all don't have AC? I thought a sophisticated cat like you would at least have a window unit."

"We do but I was cold. Sometimes I like to sit out here to see what's going on."

"Not a damn thing, that's fa sho." We sat in silence for a second. I didn't know he could be that quiet. With Trae, you never knew what he might say, or how he might embarrass you.

"Your peeps at home?"

"No, Dino's at work and Sharonda is probably at her mama's."

"Y'all got some Coke?"

"No, I need to go to the store. I believe we got some lemonade and juice. And water."

"Aight, how about some water then. I need to be drinkin' more water anyway."

He followed me inside, staying in the living room while I went into the kitchen. When I came back with the glass of ice water, Trae was standing in front of the air conditioner, rotating his head to cool his brow.

"Aight, thanks Quincy. We can go back on the porch if you want."

"No, no problem. About time to

come in anyway. Don't want to get eaten up by the mosquitos."

He paused, half-full glass in hand, looking easily around the room. "Yeah, that's one of the things I like about you. You move slow. You take it easy. I don't ever see you rushing."

I chuckled. "Too hot to rush. I guess I do take my time."

He kept looking around. "Your stuff is always neat, in order." Looked back at me. "You got yourself together. You always been together. And you live in the same 'hood' as the rest of us." We didn't live in a hard core 'hood,' but it wasn't the 'burbs,' either. Was several blocks of Black working-class people who clocked in to pay the bills, who bought houses and raised families and went to church. I just shrugged and half-smiled. He put the glass down on the *Jet* magazine on the table. "Yeah, that's what I like about you."

His first kiss was gentle, testing my surprise. His second one tasted like the sweetness of flavored tobacco. Our tongues mingled on his third one, as he cupped my cheeks with both palms, like an assurance that this was happening for real.

"Yeah, that's what I like about you."

TWO

The tour group had moved on, had left Jaylyn behind. Or at least that's how she wanted it to seem; she wasn't at all worried. She knew where she was staying, and if she couldn't speak enough Spanish to find her way back, at the very least she could write down the hotel's name to show a cab driver. It was embarrassing enough to be in a tour group, given her pride in being an independent soul, having scrimped to buy her own Baltimore condo and toiled to grow her consultancy practice. But she was a novice at traveling abroad, having only been to the Bahamas, which was an easy first step, given the same language and fact that she could almost blend in if she didn't speak.

Travel to Cuba was a different challenge altogether, and coming as part of a tour group was the only way she felt secure enough to navigate the language difference and the political mess between the two countries. Her good girlfriend Tamara was supposed to come with, but was back home recuperating from an appendectomy that happened a week before their departure.

This left Jaylyn to her own devices, which was fine, except in this tour group of 30, she was the only fly in the buttermilk. Her fellow travelers fell into two camps: the eternal spring breakers, who were out for rum, cigars, and salsa (and cheap sex, she suspected), or the culture jockeys, who constantly jousted with each other to be more knowledgeable and down-for-the-Revolution than anyone else.

And then there was her. So while she probably would catch some heat for getting "lost" (she pictured mental air quotes while she thought this), given the strict itineraries that these US/Cuba travel programs were required to stick with, she was also a grown woman practicing her citizenship in the world. Besides, her dimpled, cinnamon-skinned tour guide would probably understand, as they'd exchanged sly knowing smiles whenever the competition between the group's know-it-alls started heating up.

Yes, Eduardo would understand her.

Jaylyn strolled through the insistent din and constant motion surrounding her in Habana Vieja, the oldest part of the city. She enjoyed the colors and sounds as they exploded around her, set amidst the heavily worn—but still standing—colonial-era buildings. Fortunately, the temperature was Goldilocks pleasant—not too hot, not too muggy, just right. Jaylyn noted the rapid-fire Spanish punctuating every exchange she saw: old men gathered in a small cluster around a transistor radio as old as they were; schoolkids dressed in royal blue jumpers, white shirts, and red neckties, playfully teasing each other as they made their way home; hobbling women grasping multiple shopping bags calling out greetings while finishing errands.

A wave of joy rose in Jaylyn's chest for being part of this street rhythm, for feeling connected to her surroundings by merely being present. She walked on, allowing her steps to match the seaside syncopation of what was just another regular day in La Habana.

THREE

SHUT THE FUCK UUUUP! Marcel's entire life converged, laser-focused, into the heat of this moment. As he stood in the shocked silence, fists clenched and raised to his shoulders, mouth agape, throat raspy and burning from exertion, his pent-up pains unleashed as crisply as a champagne bottle popping.

All the transgressions rushed back into clear view, flooding his brain in a heady, potent mix with adrenaline: the constant negativity and criticism about anything he ever did or tried. Not having the space to be a kid, to play and be loud and happy, to run ragged, to allow his shirt tails to show. Not being able to scrape knees and tumble home coated in sweat and funk. Not being allowed to express himself without his truth sticking in his throat like a barely-chewed morsel.

He remembered every single slap to the face, the numbing sting and the momentary disorientation after being struck. He remembered the immediate need to hold back any tears or to stifle any cries, as the imminent threat hung in the air of a worse thrashing. He'd tried to be a perfect child, barely seen and barely heard, only to discover later that there is no such creature, no perfect child.

This was not the West Indies. Kids and families did things differently here. His parents left behind their families, their mother tongue patois, and their homeland routines and struggles, but brought an Old Testament-style discipline to this new land. Marcel was born here, and grew existing in two worlds, theirs and one that was increasingly his alone.

He couldn't exactly call himself abused or neglected, in the parlance of the social workers at his series of private schools, as he was always neatly dressed, well-fed daily, warm in winters, and well-distanced from any dangers of the outside world. But neither could he call himself loved. Theirs wasn't parental love; it was an 18-year penance for the sin of his conception, the manifestation of their lust. He secretly questioned whether they loved one another, as there were no displays of affection between them that he could recall in his lifetime. Had he even seen them kiss? Hold hands? Heard them exchange a soft word or belly-bursting laughter between them? Is that why he had no siblings?

After years of bondage under his father's bruising hands and mother's unyielding tongue, Marcel had escaped. Leaving the confines of their tight-leashed existence at first stunned his senses, was a Wizard of Oz transition from shades of grey to a brilliant technicolor, even beyond the flashes of freedom during the secondary school day. In college, he found that liberation was a practice, a muscle to exercise daily. And in it he'd found his voice, propelled by anger and a newfound discovery of self-worth, a backbone.

All this crystallized in the shock of the moment. They no longer had power over him, not physical or mental. And as far as he was concerned now, they could go to Hell. He'd found himself.

FOUR

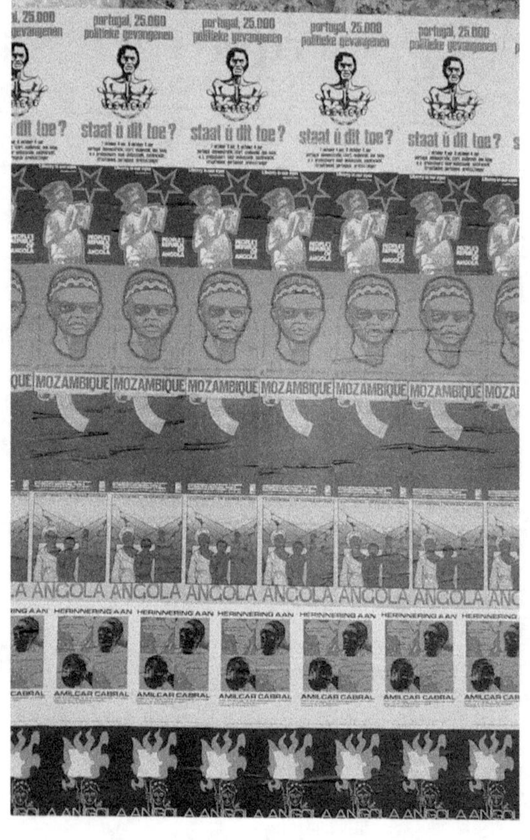

portugal, 25.000 politieke gevangenen
staat ù dit toe?
MOZAMBIQUE
ANGOLA
HERINNERING AAN
AMILCAR CABRAL
ANGOLA

Of course, I'm up for the task. The ancestors positioned me here for this very purpose, to leave a legacy of great import. Our comrade leader himself chose me for this vast undertaking, understanding that the muscles of men may vanquish opponents, but the minds of women build nations. You Westerners have a similar belief in "the hand that rocks the cradle..."

The colonizers left their marks here on our land in many ways, like mud tracks throughout a house, yes? Places had names before the colonizers' arrival and disruption. The places that were colonizer settlements—those that didn't exist beforehand—we will rename according to the character and spirit of the region.

In fact, this is the general philosophy behind our renaming programme. After all, why should we keep the shed skin of a snake? Let's rid ourselves of those ghosts, yes? The awkward mixture of indigenous and Western languages that you see dotting the maps of other nations— towns and *villes* and *praias*? We'll have none of that here, unless it's by our own volition, made allowable in remembrance of those Freedom Fighters who shunned the colonizers and took up The People's Cause.

But we have plenty of our own Freedom Fighters to begin with. There are enough things that need renaming, everything from cities to villages to the majestic mountain range in the south that nurtured the independence movement. Ironic yet righteous, isn't it, that The People's Cause was born in a place renamed by colonizers? The great mountains boasted a beautiful name, which loosely translates as "Closest to the Infinity of the Heavens", but the colonizers, displaying their typical arrogance and disregard, renamed it after their king. So their regent is more important than the omnipresence of the universe? No, that will not be allowed to stand. We don't worship their king, nor shall we remember him when standing atop the pinnacles, praising the vastness of the sky.

But as I was saying, everything needs a refresh, a rebrand. We recognize that this will cause confusion, and we are therefore planning to introduce the changes in a series of transitions. We will allow dual names for three years, after which we will move to indigenous names only. Three years is enough time to get prepared, yes?

Moreover, it is my aim to ensure that we have women's names front and center, for it was us women who fought side by side with our men to drive the colonizers back into the sea. So why should the spoils of victory all accrue to men? No, I want our herstory—a term I picked up from your Alice Walker—to be woven throughout the tapestry of our nation, just like the beautiful *akanlya* fabric that is our national dress.

Let the glory of our revolution be an everyday one; each time people call out these names, it will be a celebration of our history, our language, and our heroes, yes?

I cannot wait to begin.

FIVE

I'm only doing this because Jessica asked. And for the extra 50 pounds, of course. I've never thought myself the type to model. Jess says I'm "proper fit," says I "got those good Ashanti genes," whatever that means. I'm a decent-looking bruv, started working out regularly while at university, and try to eat healthy and all that. Hard to maintain a deep love for jollof and keep a decent waistline, yeah?

Sometimes Jess calls me Plum. At first, I found it rather annoying, a lazy and obvious nickname, but now it ain't so bad. I mean, it might feel different if she said, "my Plum" or "my tasty Plum," although if I were to choose, it would be "my big

Aubergine." But I don't think she has that kind of intention about us, so I've gotten used to the occasional "Plum." Fortunately, I didn't experience any of that African-Booty-Scratcher kind of teasing when I was a kid; my family lived in Kumasi before I came back to Lewisham for Year 10. I didn't have that kind of dark-skinned shaming thing that some of my other mates did. I know it's different for girls, what with the whole skin bleaching thing still in vogue. The hands and ankles are the giveaways—if a girl has a tan face but cocoa hands or ankles, she's definitely lightening up. Strange, but who am I to judge? My two sisters are followers of Chimamanda Adichie, so they don't bother with the kind of oppressive stuff they'd call a Eurocentrist male gaze and all.

Speaking of the male gaze, the tables are turned today. I guess Jess has that kind of power over me, otherwise I never would've pictured myself sitting here starkers at this girlfriends' night out. They're doing a wine-and-sip, a loony idea that Jess picked up from a You Tube video from some girls in New York. What's odder still is that there's another dude, another so-called model in the room, which makes all this a bit awkward, yeah? It does lessen the embarrassment of having all eyes on me, but still feels very strange. Fortunately, we're not facing one another. Fortunately, I'm sitting down so that all of my bits (which aren't so itty bitty, thank you very much) aren't just bobbing about. That could be a problem. But I shouldn't think about that; I should stay focused on milder things like puppies and nuns.

Most of the girls are actually painting, now that they got past the initial giggling and such. Jess told me it would probably be less, ermmm, stimulating for me if I don't make eye contact while posing, but I am curious to see some of the work—how does a roomful of black women see me, completely exposed and vulnerable before them?

I probably shouldn't waste this opportunity, yeah? Maybe I'll chat up some of the ladies—once dressed, of course. Imagine getting a date outta this—what would Jess think of ol' Plum then?

SIX

"**G**irl, Black might be beautiful, but you done done it now." June glanced past herself in the mirror at Mae standing wide-eyed behind her. June refocused on herself; kept patting her tight curls into a neat oval.

"I don't see what the big deal is."

June tried to be matter-of-fact, but the butterflies in her stomach were as bad as they sometimes got before a big race. If Mae, her roommate, teammate, and closest friend thought she was in the wrong, no telling what others would think. But June needed to do what she needed to do.

She had always hated the stench of searing hair as it was pulled through the pressing comb. She did enjoy the Saturday night ritual with her mother, sisters, aunts, and eventually her good girlfriends as they prepared their hair for the week to come, sitting around gossiping and laughing about think-they-grown woman stuff while fiddling with pomade, rollers, and bobby pins. She just didn't want to put her own hair through those pains anymore. So, when the brother came through campus selling handmade wooden hair picks, she bought one with a bit of her "hamburger money," as her daddy called the small allowance he sent to her every month.

She didn't tell anybody, just quietly kept the pick wrapped in a handkerchief in her panty drawer, where Mae wouldn't run across it while occasionally rummaging through to borrow something here or there. June made up her mind over three months, first after hearing Stokely Carmichael speak, then after reading an article in *Ebony*, then coming across the hawker. June quit pressing her hair, cut off the straight ends, and in the aftermath, she thought it looked pretty, framing her face and roundish features the way it did. It felt so soft and springy—natural, just like the name.

Mae was right, though. Now came the reckoning. She would have to face Coach Temple. June felt she could handle anybody else, but Coach Temple was only a few steps behind Jesus in her book. "Foxes, not oxes!" she could hear him thundering. "I,

for one, do not think that I am an ox,"
June thought.

She wondered if he'd send her back
home so her parents could judge her for
themselves, shunned and shamed for
her turn toward those Black radicals.
June wasn't a rebel; she trained hard
in practice, was a disciplined and fine
student, and had never been a sassy or
back-talking type. June was proud to
be a Tigerbelle, and while she didn't
possess the talent of Wilma, Wyomia,
or Edith, she didn't want to mar the
team's reputation.

June turned to Mae, whose full name
was Etta Mae, but because she and
June were peas in a pod since meeting
their first year in college, everybody

took to calling them Mae and June. "Well, ain't nothin' to it but to do it." June wrapped her head in a scarf, grabbed her bag, and went off to meet Coach Temple.

SEVEN

The paddle dipped and pushed through the slick crystal water. Zeke nodded and let loose a low register hum that vibrated in his upper chest, like he'd just tasted something wonderful. "Mmmm." He steered further from shore, a narrow strip of sand that provided an easy access point to the river as it wound through the bright green foothills. He'd never kayaked on this river in this otherwise landlocked part of the state; the first time he was here, he'd pulled off the road searching for a place to just sit and watch the river's slow crawl. The presence of paddlers was a pleasant invitation to him to return.

He'd taken up kayaking years ago after an initial group outing; for him it had turned into a solitary pursuit and pleasure, a physical meditation of sorts, like running. Otherwise he didn't think of himself as an outdoorsy guy, and still saw these spaces as occupied by Cliff Bar-eating white dudes driving Subarus and pickup trucks. He felt awkward and uncomfortable around those adventure types, instead seeing himself more like storybook Native Americans, quietly navigating their canoes through the thoroughfares of their territory.

Zeke was drawn to kayaking because it allowed him to be close to the water without actually being submerged in it. He'd kayaked on bays, estuaries, lakes, and even several occasions in the choppy saltwater of a large bay. He'd once tried the ocean but since he wasn't a good swimmer, he was too intimidated to paddle into the strong surf. Gentle water like this is perfect. While it could kick up and be playful, it was mostly as peaceful and soothing as bathwater.

Zeke settled into a slow rhythm while paddling. Strains of a spiritual came to him like a cliché, but a welcomed one. He thought of verse John 5:4, "For an angel went down at a certain season into the pool and troubled the water." Zeke wasn't wading, but he too felt healed.

Most other thoughts fell away as he guided the plastic hull through the upstream current near the middle of the river. With each paddle stroke, his shoulders were freed from the yoke of everyday stress: relationship questions and financial concerns, national politics and office politicking. He wasn't the type to move through life without regard to immediate and long-term potential dangers; in fact, he considered himself to be too risk averse. "But here I am, a Black man out on the water. That's risky!" He chuckled. Times like these, surrounded by natural beauty and being physically exerted just enough to feel enlivened but not exhausted, filled him with gratitude.

He breathed deeply and began another low hum, remembering

the lyrics to another hymn from his church upbringing: "When peace like a river, attendeth my way, when sorrows like sea billows roll. Whatever my lot, thou hast taught me to say, it is well, it is well, with my soul." With that, Zeke continued upriver, as easy as the light breeze accompanying him.

EIGHT

CHICAGO

Okay, quick check. I got my mashed yams, my garlic greens, my cayenne cornbread, my cauliflower wings—there's the BBQ, there's the ranch—my black-eyed pea patties, my "mac and cheers," my chocolate mousse—it's made with avocados, shhh, don't tell nobody—and my carrot and honey cupcakes. I'm still experimenting with my pinto bean burger recipe, so we'll bring that out here next year. Gotta get 'em right or word'll spread all throughout Washington Park that Nzinga's bean patties are dry! HaHAAA! We can't have that, no we can't! Right?!

It took a couple of years for us to really get going but once the word got out that my food was da bomb diggity, it's like yellow jackets at a picnic—can't keep 'em off ya! Wherever we go, whatever street festival or parade or tailgating, the people keep on coming! CaCHING! Hahahaha!

But don't get me wrong, I'm not just about these coins; I see myself as bringing a public service to my community, that yes, we CAN eat great soul food and not have it kill us. RIGHT? Yes we CAN! Yes we CAN! And speaking of yes we can, chile, I sure do miss having OUR First Family in the White House. Right? South Side in the Houuuuuse! Yes we COULD and yes we DID! HaHAAA!

Okay so, where was I? Okay, baby,

here, make yourself double useful while you're listening to me and please put those boxes of plates and stuff in the van; they're not too heavy. We're trying some bamboo products this year, more sustainable so all that plastic and styrofoam doesn't end up in the Lake! Or down in Gary buried under somebody's backyard, you know what I'm saying? We can do better because we KNOW better, right? RIGHT.

Okay, I think that's about it. We'll get all this food loaded up and ready to roll. I think this is gonna be our last year setting up a booth and not using the food truck. The booth gives us more space and doesn't get as hot, but I sure am proud of my truck! Ain't it pretty? My nephew created the design; he's a student at the Art Institute and we are very, VERY proud of him! He helped with all of our branding, our look. I wanted something bright and Black—and he delivered! Look at this—how he made this little kente stripe of soul food! Ain't that cute? And that's just what we're about— style AND substance! Right? RIGHT. I mean, I want people to get good food and good service! We can't be looking raggedy; can't be acting foul! No, at Nzinga's you are going to get service with a smile! No excuse for not being pleasant. We may be from the Chi, but everybody here got roots in Mississippi, chile. I'm bringing you Midwestern practicality with Southern hospitality! YES!

Okay let's see—that's about it! Let's roll! Got a long day ahead of us! ChaCHING haHAA!

NINE

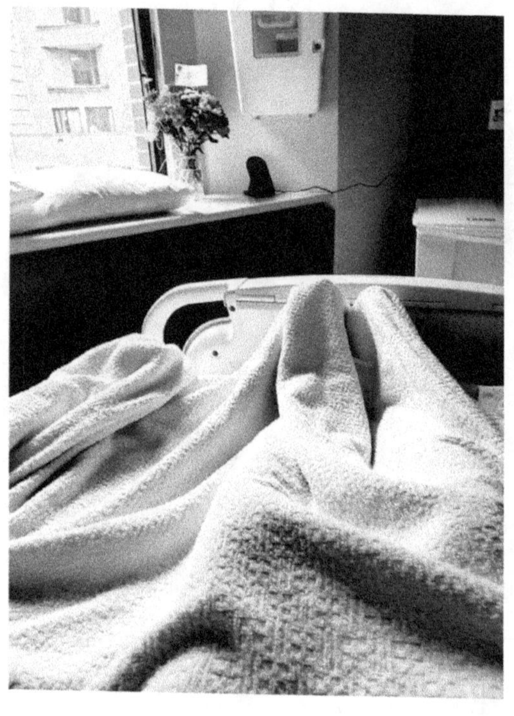

Does fear have the power to melt? I wonder. Lately when I've come out of sleep, I've felt multiple sensations—first a groggy recognition that I'm awake. Then the soreness from the wound. Then the wave of fresh dread rolling through my body. Maybe it's an adrenaline rush, since I can so vividly feel the heat seeping into my limbs from the burning furnace here in my belly. Then I feel hot and very afraid and very weak, which is why I think this is like melting. And if I stay in this state for too long, my body will likely break like glass into a million tiny shards, or it'll liquify into a big lumpy brown puddle, soaking through these sheets and this mattress. Might not be a bad way to go. But at this moment I can't consider images and ideas like that; I have to keep my mind set on healing.

When my sense of humor kicks in, she tells me, "Nina, there are plenty of one-breasted womyn roaming the Earth. You're not the first or the final." She makes me want to adorn war paint and find my tribe, other one-boobed — or none-boobed! – sisters all wearing cargo pants and leather messenger bags slung over one shoulder to emphasize the flat empty space(s) on our chests. A real band of warriors! Some of us have hair and some are bald, by chemo or by choice. We'll march together and comfort each other and question why we need to cover our top halves in the first place, like breasts are some sort of indecent insult to mankind. If men don't want anything to stare at, teach 'em not to stare!

Thinking like that helps me get it together, helps me to pull back from melting into the big brown puddle. It's an everyday journey, because sometimes I consider this mastectomy as a symbol of the state of the world, that things dearly and closely held to me are being snatched away, that there's an ominous force at work in the background that eats away at self-actualization until it kills the spirit. And I can't give in. I must soldier on (there we go again with the war imagery!).

I once heard a speaker say that we

must find the thing in ourselves that is bigger than fear and use it as our source and shield. Or maybe they said "sword and shield," but I'm tired of these war symbols, so I'm going to say "source." This that is happening to me is not the end of the world. I use humor as my source, but also gratitude for my blessings, that I love and am loved, that bitterness has never been my cup of tea.

My honeypie will be over to see me soon to help me up, to sit and hold my hand, to keep me smiling (too sore to laugh yet), to keep me generating my source of strength, to keep me from dissolving into nothing.

TEN

There's no perfect way to describe this...it's way different than anything i could have imagined or was taught...it's simultaneously being everywhere and not having to go from place to place...you think it and you're there...i shouldn't say "think"... there is no more thinking, not in the cognitive sense because, well, you're no longer bound by a body...and the ways that you're accustomed to feeling physical aches and pains...how emotions show up as belly knots or tears springing from your eyes...none of that applies anymore....

again, i don't quite have words to capture it, but like the stylistics said, you are everything, and everything is, well, us...it's like everything reverts to the very beginning...truly ashes to ashes, dust to dust...all atomized and recast on a cosmic scale...you instantly become a molecular part of all that has ever existed...

and even more amazing, once that happens, the precise order of the universe becomes crystal clear, like you've inherited the sum of knowledge of the ages...it's ironic that the meaning of life is revealed at this point...and you learn that the so many of the things that bound or restrained us in human form are silly, are absolutely trivial...the limitations and deep cruelties inflicted upon each other were never, ever necessary...

armed with this new clarity, you may

find yourself wanting to help those who still exist as before, to warn them of oncoming turbulence or protect them from pain or even conjure up a blessing or two for them, but it's near impossible to re-cross the realm in any recognizable form...yet because you are everywhere, those who are listening can hear you, can feel your omnipresence...

but no, there's no returning as a guardian angel...why would you want to...why go backwards...there is no backward movement in this plane... no forward movement either, not like you have grown accustomed to...the rush and never-ending quest for the next thing, big or small, accomplished or acquired...no need for all that, since all of our needs are met because, well, there are no needs...again, you are part of everything, and truly understand that everything is life...

what you now think of as "dead" is a misnomer because you don't simply cease to exist...maybe a single discrete being, yes...but your energy continues on...you transform into an eternal and hyper-connected and exponentially bigger energy than anything you can imagine, even with me talking to and through you now...it's better than all the hymns and chants and holy day promises combined...but be forewarned...it's not streets of gold and long white robes...not the fabled milk and honey and seeing all the loved ones you missed so much over the years, even though they're out here too...you're actually closer to them now than ever before...they're everywhere and everything too....

get ready...and as practice, love as much as you can...love everything beautiful...be sure to notice the color purple in a field somewhere haha... try to see the life in everything, everyone...live as inspired as you can... yes, that's good practice...because this is something else...truly on a whole 'nother level....

THE END

Thanks to Derek, Dion, Greg, Rebekah, and Sonya for your help and encouragement.

CEDRIC BROWN is the author of *Eyes of Water & Stone: From Havana with Love* and *Tar Heel Born: A Native Son Speaks on Race, Religion, & Reconciliation*. His work is also included in the anthologies *Blacktino Queer Performance* and *The Road Before Us: 100 Black Gay Poets*. Cedric is the founder of the Jacobs/Jones African American Literary Prize, sponsored by the North Carolina Writers Network, and co-founder of the Randall Kenan Prize for Black LGBTQ Fiction, sponsored by Lambda Literary Foundation. He lives in Winston-Salem, North Carolina, USA.

PHOTOS

All photos by Cedric Brown
except where noted.

ONE: Winston-Salem, NC. April 2020.

TWO: Havana, Cuba. January 2002.

THREE: By Frances Coch December 2017.

FOUR: Lisbon, Portugal. July 2025.

FIVE: Palm Springs, CA. May 2025.

SIX: Winston-Salem, NC. Circa 1965.
Photographer unknown

SEVEN: Pittsboro, NC. September 2023.

EIGHT: Chicago, IL. July 2018.

NINE: Winston-Salem, NC. May 2022.

TEN: Los Angeles, CA. October 2019.

Junie's
Mood
Press

PO Box 17506

Winston-Salem, NC 27106

USA

None of this work was generated by

Artificial Intelligence.

9 780985 700669